James Brown

Poems, songs & recitations in the Lancashire dialect

James Brown

Poems, songs & recitations in the Lancashire dialect

ISBN/EAN: 9783337175993

Printed in Europe, USA, Canada, Australia, Japan

Cover: Foto ©Andreas Hilbeck / pixelio.de

More available books at **www.hansebooks.com**

POEMS, SONGS, & RECITATIONS

IN THE LANCASHIRE DIALECT.

——————

By JAMES BROWN,

HAIGH.

——————

WIGAN:
PRINTED BY R. PLATT, 2, STANDISHGATE,
1881.

To

The Rt. Honble. the Earl of Crawford & Balcarres,

Lord Lindsay,

&c.

CONTENTS.

LANCASHIRE POEMS.

NEAW PEGGY DUNNOD TAWK THAD WA."

NEAW Peggy lass id winnod do,
  For thee to tawk thad way;
Id welly breks mi hert i' two,
  Do howd thi din aw pray;
Whod ever arto thinkin on?
  Heaw conto serv mi so?
Hav'no aw bin a faithfu mon?
  Just ax thi brother Joe.

Ween nod mich brass owd luv thads troo,
   Bud then wi toime un care ;
Iv thee un me together poo,
   Wi' may hev un to spare.
Aw dunnod think ud wi shall be
   Loike sum foonk, clemmed un cowd ;
Becose awst gi' mi wage to thee,
   For't cheer us wen we're owd.

Cum Peggy neaw, un led's ged wed,
   Tha'll never roo aw know ;
Un iv ween meawths sent to bi fed,
   Aw'll wark hard for um o',
No deawt wi shall hev two or three,
   For't feed besoide cawr own ;
Still never moind aw shannod spree,
   Bud cum reet whoam upth' lone.

Best thing owd derlin wi con do,
   Ist' help each other on ;
A looad is leeter borne bi two,
   Nor wen its borne wi one.
Trouble may cum wi connod tell,
   Id plagues booath hee un low ;
Bud iv aw con feight throo' misel,
   Aw'll nod hurt thee ud o'.

Un iv we're poor we'll nod lament,
  Nor enry nobrey's lot ;
Bud pray ud peace un sweet content,
  May dwell within cawr cot.
Then wen loife's struggles here are o'er,
  Aw hope wi o' mi hert,
Ud wi mun meet on thad breet shore,
  Wheer gud fooak never pert.

Well John, aw loike o' uds bin sed,
  To me this very nect ;
So neaw aw'll promise to bi wed,
  Un mak thy sad hert leet.
Pudth' axins up to morn mi lad,
  There's nowt ul be amiss.
Aw will mi lass un bi reet glad,
  Lets seeal id wi a kiss.

THE ROYAL VISIT TO WIGAN
(JUNE, 1873).

HAVIN' a bit o' leighshure toime,
 Aw'll just sit deawn an' pen a rhoime,
Abeawt that greight hospishus day
Which Wiggin shortly will display.

On th' third o' June aw understand,
Th' owd burro' will bi deckd' quoite grand,
An nowt bud reet, for on that day,
A Royal pair will visit Haigh.

Wheer eawr respected Earl, aw know,
Will on their Highnesses bestow,
Thoose good things money con procure,
To mak' their happiness secure.

Yo' should see th' vast preparashuns,
Up ud th' Ho an' throo th' plantashuns;
Besides the noble House o' Haigh,
Will feast some hundreds on thad day.

Leds cheer booath Lord an' Lady C.,
For helpin' on th' Infirmary;
Their koindly akshuns, awve no deawt,
Hav' browt this grand event abeawt.

Becose, wi me yo'll o agree,
Thad they invoited Royalty,
Afther th' Wiggin Corporashun
Had sent up their depitashun.

Awm shure cawr wealthy worthy Mayor *
Every good thing will prepare,
For th' Royal guests, an' th' rest o'th' bunch,
Thad he intends axin to lunch.

His spred ull boath bi rich an' grand,
Becose he's money at command ;
Aw'll bet a shillin' to a groat
He's cash enough to sink a boat.

Awm gradely glad thad Mesther Simm
Eawr able chief, ull dine wi him ;
His wurship's very koind indeed,
For thus invitin' him to feed.

Moi word, ther'll be a bonny stur,
Foak lookin' eawt nd every dur ;
Greight multytudes ull sheawt an' sing
For th' Prince o' Wales, cawr futer King.

May He who gurverns up abuv,
Breathe on the Royal pair His luv,
An' send th' owd sun to shed his rays,
Throocawt cawr laud on thoose three days.

* N. Eckersley, Esq., J.P.

Iv we're bless'd wi pleasant weather,
Led us o' unoite together,
An' thank th' Creator uv cawr frame,
For koindly sendin' us the same.

So, neaw, aw'll bid yo o' adew,
Aw think awve written loines enoo,
An' afther th' busy stur is o'er,
Iv awve spare toime, aw'll tell yo more.

TH' HAIGH HO' BANQUET AN' TH' WIGGIN DECORASHUNS.

A W sed last wick, wen th' stur wur o'er,
  Iv aw'd spare toime, aw'd tell yo more ;
So whoile awre nothin' else to do,
Aw'll tak' mi pen an' buckle to.

Fust thing just let mi tel yo o',
Aw're axt to th' banquet ud Haigh Ho ;
An' raly, foak, beawt ony puff,
Aw never tasted better stuff.

Th' tables wur spred so rich an' foine,
Aw felt aw're cuttin' quoite a shoine,
An' lots besoide aw soon could name,
Ud very loikly felt the same.

One thing aw'll say, an' thads not two,
We'd o' a reglar jolly do ;
An' whod wur th' best, aw yerd th' Earl say,
" Awm glad to meet yo here to-day."

Yo connod tell heaw quare aw went
Wen th' Lord an' th' Lady coom i'th' tent,
An' stood so very close to me,
I'th' front o' Mesther Majendie.

Who ably o'er us did presoide,
An' spoke koind words on every side ;
Aw end no' help but often gaze
Upon his pleasant smoilin' face.

A word for th' Genral, then aw've done,
Becose, yo know, aw mon pass on,
Or else aw never shall get throo
Whod awm intendin' for to do.

They're lots o' foak thad day i'th' place
Reet glad to see his gallant face ;
Let's hope he'll live long to command
His army in a foreign land.

Neaw, awm off throo th' Haigh plantashuns
For t' see Wiggin decorashuns ;
An' as aw pass the streets aw'll view,
An' render praise wheer id is due.

Aw'll stert at top o'th' Standishgate,
There's Mesther Leigh's heawse looks fust-rate
Then th' Royal Oak an' th' Scarisbrick Arms,
Hav' booath little bits o' charms.

Hilton, Dean, an' Pendlebury,
Each hav' drest their place quoite merry ;
Birkett, wi' Evans an' McClure,
Had been busy aw feel quoite sure.

Taylor, Entwistle, Platt, au' th' Bank,
Will each among the others rank ;
An' Mesther Whitfield's done his share,
Theerfore aw'll use each perty fair.

Messrs. Coop, wi' th' Meck's also,
Hev' made their places quoite a show ;
Wheer tother's one thank, gi' these two,
Or else they'll never ged their due.

Hesketh, at th' Minorca Hotel,
Has made his place look pretty well ;
An' Mrs. Fogg, across the street,
Has also made the Clarence neat.

Th' proprietors o'th' District Bank,
Deserve a rare good thumpin' thank,
For their grand illuminashuns,
Which hav' caused greight preparashuns.

There's Gregson, Duff, an' cawr Teawn Clerk,
Each fixt things up to shoine wen derk ;
No deawt these perties did their best,
An' deserve praise just same as th' rest.

Jim Hilton, Cookson, an' th' Beehive,
Hav' made their shops look o' alive ;
Raly foak, they're aw three pretty,
An' noice enoof for Lunnon city.

Th' last two places are Gee an' Wright,
Each one presents a splendid sight ;
Aw welly dust bet yo' a creawn,
These two are th' best i' Wiggin teawn.

So neaw id's toime for me to stop,
Or yo'll nod foind these lines a shop ;
Wen awre coed ud th' Exhibishun,
Yo' shall have a third edishun.

Iv awre forgetten two or three,
Aw hope yo'll koindly excuse me ;
An' should this piece be incorrect,
Remember this— no one's perfect.

A VISIT TO TH' EXHIBISHUN.

AST Monday neet, just afther tay,
   Aw bang'd reet off tort Wiggin way,
An' paid a shillin' for admishun,
Into eawr grand Exhibishun.

Next thing aw bowt a book at th' dur,
An' paid th' chap sixpence beawt demur,
Becose yo mit as weel keep cawt
As goo i sich loike places beawt.

Then off aw scet throo th' bottom room,
Wheer Peck an' Sons fix't up their loom ;
An' scores o things wur to be seen,
Includin' thoose thad workt bi steam.

Th' best thing thad did my fancy tak'
Wur th' engine made bi Tummus Brack,
A cliver mon, as yo' will see,
An' works for th' Top Place Company.

Greight praise is due, each one will say,
Thad does this specimun survey ;
It shows boath yung an' owd loikewoise,
Wot cou bi done by enterproise.

Other models wur theer on view,
From Pemberton, Whoite Moss, an' Crewe,
Which aw thowt lookt very fair ;
Still, th' best would not wi Brack's compare.

George Hoskin's lad wen but eighteen,
Made two engines thad workt by steam ;
These also stood upon a stage,
An' lookt fust-rate for one his age.

Next, Peter Johnson, sent a stock,
O' baw's turnt cawt o' solid block ;
Wich specimuns aw thowt wur good,
Altho' formt cawt o' nowt but wood.

Then other friends sent models too ;
Aw think aw'd betther name a few ;
Theerfore iv yo'll giv' attenshun,
A toothrey on 'em aw will menshun.

Tom Yates, ith Scowse, au engine sent,
Wich to dispose of he was bent :
An' George Roby wi' John Wilcock,
Each added one also to th' stock.

The Wigan Coal and Iron Co.,
Showed an attracktive one also ;
Made from Crawford Pits, one an' two,
An' fitted up complete o' throo.

Rideawt, fro Standish Papper Mill,
Exhibited some works of skill ;
One, a gauge for measurin plate,
An' lots besoide aw could relate.

N. Eckersley, thad good owd name,
Subscroibed a little throstle frame ;
A piece o' work wich aw've no deawt,
His koind feyther thowt mich abcawt.

Littler, an' Wilkinson also,
Hav' each sent models for to show ;
And Brothers Coupe, of Worsley Mesnes,
Some good work sent fort spred their names.

The Pepper Mill Brass Foundry Co.,
Wurnod for bein' done ud o';
Ther case o' brass lookt very noice,
An' would hav' fotched a greight hee proice.

Messrs. Rowland an' Makinson,
Hav' done as mich as ony one ;
If aw wur wuth wot these two sent
Aw'd spend six months ou th' continent.

In a corner wich aw did pass,
A mon wur busy blowin' glass ;
Into ornayments wi a leet,
Wich process aw thowt quite a treat.

Rooms one an' two lookt very foine,
Wheer aw see Tasker's foreign coin ;
An' o' thoose other noice things too,
Wich Shortrede's lady had ou view.

Next reawm to these it fairly swarms,
Wi pistols, guns, an' other arms ;
Wich things aw dunnot care abeawt,
Tho they're useful sometoimes no deawt.

Eh, wot picturs ther wur on view,
They filled two rooms an' th' staircase too ;
Th' mooast of wich aw think com from
Th' Earl o' Derby an' John Thom.

T. P. Stuart an' Edward Scott,
Koindly sent a numerous lot ;
An' Holt shows one by T. R. Lowe,
Wich is worthy of note also.

Lord Lindsay nearly fills a room,
Wi' things belongin' th' sun an moon ;
Ony that does these understand,
Witheawt a deawt will say they're grand.

Tho' awve plenty i' mi yed,
Aw'd better stop, enoof's bin sed ;
Iv aw wur't tell yo wot aw know,
Yoar papper wud na howd it o'.

So neaw mi pertin' words shall be,
Success to cawr Infirmary ;
An' may it prove a place o' rest,
Unto the helpless and distrest.

LINES ON A VISIT TO A FRIEND
AT BURSCOUGH.*

OWD friend ! aw never shal forged,
   Mi trip last new yer's day ;
To thy grand heawse wheer things wur spread,
   So plentiful an' gay.

Awve co'd on friends, ay' mony o score,
   Bud never har' aw met ;
Wi one uds trayted me afore,
   Loike thee an' thy owd pet.

I'd fill'd mi hert brimful o' glee,
   To meet wi sich glad cheer ;
A mon loike thee shud never dee,
   Bud live on yer bi yer.

God bless thi lad, an' th' woife also,
   Loikewise thi childer too' ;
May health an' peace attend yo' o,
   Whoile th' world tha travels throo.

Tha's risked thi loife o'er th' stormy seas,
   An' met wi rare success ,
Throo sellin' bacon, lard, an' cheese,
   Greight wealth tha does possess.

* Henry Ellis, Esq.

Aw know tha's mony o' theawsand peawnd
   An' wish tha'd ten toimes more ;
Then tha could buy a lump o' greawnd,
   For thee an' me t' shoot o'er.

Thoose friends o' thoine shud come agen,
   We'd har' some jolly fun ;
Aw know they'd grin for t' see two men,
   Loike us wi each a gun.

Becose aw connod shoot a bit
   An' happly tha'd bith same ;
They'd soon tell me aw wurnod fit
   For ony sich loike game.

Bud then whods use, aw shudno care,
   A rap chus whod they said ;
Iv tha knock'd o'er a brid or hare,
   On which aw could be fed.

Aw watch'd thi oft thad afternoon,
   Tha look'd so merry lad ;
When Lathom band play'd cawt a tune,
   I'd made me doance loike mad.

Bud wurnd aw vex'd to hear some thief,
   Had crept i'th heawse throo th' fowd ;
And stole a greight big lump o' beef,
   So darin an' so bowd.

Aw wish aw'd bin at back o'th dur,
    Wen he wur gooin cawt,
For t' just giv him a run bar purr,
    Or else a rattlin cleawt.

Still never moind chap isno' free,
    Although he geet away ;
There's one abuv thad trick did see,
    He'll hav' to face some day.

So neaw aw'll close this bit oth lay,
    An' hope tha'll hav' mi o'er ;
Ud Mount Pellier on new yer's day,
    Eighteen seventy-four.

COMPOSED FOR A BIRTHDAY
CELEBRATION AT HINDLEY.

FRIEND Shuttleworth some toime ago,
   Axt me for't just giv' him a co';
On th' day wen his adopted son,
Attaint the age ov twenty-one.

I thankt him for the invitashun,
To the birthday celebrashun,
An seein' his moind wur fermly bent,
Aw reddily did giv' konsent.

Th' woife sed same neet aw're easy led,
Aye lass, ur aw should ne'er bin wed;
Moi wurd wen aw sed that to hur,
Hoo did kick up a bonny stur.

But 'twur no use aw didn't care,
Yo mon let wimmen tawk ther share;
Its foolishness to be yed strung,
Yo connot stop a woman's tung.

Neaw ladies, bless yo, do excuse,
Aw've noan cum heere yo to abuse;
Nor ony unkoind wurd to say,
On J. H. Shuttleworth's burthday.

We've met togethur at this place,
Eawr good friend's table for to grace ;
Theerfore let peace un luv aboide,
Whoile over us he does presoide.

An' as aw've bin invoited heere,
Aw'll do mi best to cause sum cheer,
An my friend Scaife ul mak yo grin,
Besoide playin' on th' violin.

He acts a quack doctor fust rate,
Iv yoan noan yerd him its a trayte ;
The characters he plays so well,
That few ith loine con him excel.

We've also getten Mesthur Pass,
Whoa understonds musick fust class ;
Awm towd he leeads a foine string band,
Which few con equal in the land.

Aw've never yerd him play mi'sel,
Tho' awm informt he con do well ;
Aw see hees browt an instrument,
On which to play is his intent.

A wurd or two an' then aw've done,
To eawr good host's adopted son ;
Whoa aw wur towd the other day,
Had proved to him a constant stay.

May he liv' for yers to come,
An' in the same course still keep on ;
Not forgettin' wen gainin' gowd,
His foster parents wen they're owd.

Awm towd, but whether its true or no,
He's keepin' company wi Miss Lowe ;
An' moor nor that aw've yerd it sed,
It'll noan be lung afore they're wed.

Wen th' day arroives friends, aw've no deawt,
Thoose whoa live heere will clear cawt ;
An' let the luvin' bride step in,
Hur change ov loife for to begin.

Lets hope 'twill be a happy one,
And that ere lung she'll hav' a son ;
Or else a pratty dowter dear,
Then wi con howd a kessunin heere.

Aw wish um booath health, wealth, an' peace,
Until ther wurldly laburs cease,
An' wen their race on earth is o'er,
Lets hope they'll meet to part no more.

COMPOSED AND RECITED AT THE
OPENING OF
INCE SUBSCRIPTION BOWLING GREEN.

FRIEND Percy axt me some toime back,
    A toothrey Lancashire loines to mak
Fort' giv' at th' openin' of cawr green,
One o'th' bigst ut ever wur seen.

So if yo'll listen for a whoile,
Aw'll neaw attempt i' merry stoile ;
Some little matters to relate,
Which deawtless yo'll appreciate.

One neet four men together met,
An' whoile they o'er ther glasses set,
A noble thowt popt in one's yed,
An' thus to tother three he sed.

Let's goo in for a bowin' green,—
Apert from th' public-heawse, aw mean,
In order that the workin' class,
May meet and play beawt spendin' brass.

To which they quickly did agree,
An' coed a meetin' at once throo me,
On the ninth ov last December,
Which some ov yo' no deawt remember.

'Twas in an office, koindly lent,
By cawr respected president,
Wen officers wur fixt upon,
To carry the worthy prodgekt on.

An' raly, friends, aw mon confess,
Ther work's bin creawnt wi' rare success ;
Greight praise to um is shurely due,
For th' manner they've carried their object throo.

Some har' laburt hard aw know,
But then one connot think ov o ;
R. Christopher, an' Nixon too
Hav' perform't abuv ther due.

Then Percy, wi Holden as well,
Hav' done far more than aw con tell ;
But Halliwell wur late at th' start,
An's not had toime to do his part.

Besides awm tow'd he couldn't get bricks,
Which placed him in a regular fix ;
Heawever friends, whoile sittin' here,
Just give these five a herty cheer.

We've also had friends far un woide,
Sendin' money on every soide ;
These are entitled to greight praise,
For helpin' us cawr funds to raise.

An' iv yo'll koindly giv' attenshun,
One or two aw'll try to menshun ;
Keepin' back lots who've given foive peawnds,
Then yo'll get sooner on the play greawnds.

Lord Crawford awm very glad to say,
Has promist twenty-foive peawnds to-day ;
A similar sum's bin gien also,
By the Wiggin Coal un Iron Co.

*Eawr president next yo'll understond,
Subscribed wi a liberal hond ;
A sum aw loike to tell agen,
Becose its hondsome, ten peawnds ten.

Lord Lindsay an' Majendie, M.P.,
Sent foive peawnds each as yo' will see ;
On reference to this little book,
If ony one's incloint to look.

W. H. Hewlett's given the same,
An' Bryham, a minin' engineer of fame;
Wi Peace cawr company's law protectur,
An' J. T. Fitzadam, a directur.

Also two more which aw shall name,
Whoa koindly subscroibed the same;
Charles Parker, Esq., of Lunnon teawn,
An' Williams, coal ageants of reneawn.

Alfred Hewlett, Esq., J.P.

Others hav' sent foire peawnds each too,
But as they're not well known to you,
An' this bein' cawr openin' day,
Aw'll name no more, yo'll want to play.

So neaw, i' biddin' yo' adew.
Mi partin' words shall be to you,
Let peace an' friendship ever abound
Both on the green and quoitin' ground.

By doin' so we shall gain friends,
Who will assist to meet cawr ends,
And abur o', to close this rhoime,
Never bowl in yoar employer's toime.

COMPOSED AND RECITED AT AN ENTERTAINMENT IN AID OF THE FUNDS OF PENNINGTON GREEN CRICKET CLUB, ASPULL.

LADIES an' gentlemen, iv yo'll just giv' attenshun
 A few simple lines aw'll neaw try to menshun ;
Koncernin' this Cricket Club, which yo' mun know,
For th' want o' sum funds ar' just neaw very low.

Ith' fust place their greawnd's noan fit to play on,
Theerfore let us render some help iv wi' con ;
They'll feel gradely glad iv its only a bit,
'Cose aw know ev'ry member is anxious to flit.

There's lots o' good greawnd abeawt Pennington Green
Belungs to a mon who aw know is'nt mean ;
Friend Beazer, no deawt would, iv axt very nice,
Do his best for to get um some at a low price,

From Mesthur R. Leigh, who wi liberal hand,
Has given for ever a portion o' land ;
Wheeron a new church will soon be erected,
For which he deserves to be highly respected.

An' aw think wen he's towd these yung lads are o' poor
He'll oppen his hert an' do a bit moor,
Toart helpin' forward that excellent game,
Which is played far an' wide bi men ov greight fame.

Aw've belunged to Haigh Club for twelve yers iv
    not moor,
Though aw've done nothin' mich beside umpire an
    scoor;
George Holme neaw an' then's put mi deawn in a
    match,
Still he knew o'th' same time aw could do nowt but
    catch.

Heawever, Albert Holker says my owdest son,
For his good play this season a proize bat has won;
Although in th' last match he had very bad luck,
As yo'd see he was bowled by Bill Bird for a duck.

Notwithstondin', th' club's efforts awm glad to confess,
Have met wi' a very fair share of success;
Becose friends, so sure as aw stond here aloive
Eawt ov fivteen good matches they've only lost foive.

Theerfore, yo'll admit they're entitled to praise,
Instead ov which let us endeavour to raise,
A sum which will pay when th' next season comes
    reawnd,
For what's badly wanted—a fresh piece o' greawnd.

Their very best thanks are awready due,
To every manager belongin' this schoo' ;
Which aw understond has koindly bin lent,
Until they are able to get a new tent.

They're greatly indebted to Jim Gibson also,
For his koindness in lendin' this grand piano ;
An' Harry Whittaker's sent some refreshments for
      nowt,
Otherwise dun yo' see they'd hev had to bin bowt.

For sich wormherted friends in these toimes of greight
      need,
Ev'ry member's occashun to feel preawd indeed ;
An' aw think there are moor abeawt here o'th' same
      sort,
Ut only want axin' to help on their sport.

Mesthur John Leigh, up at Gidlow Ho'
Is a noice little mon, which lots on yo' know ;
An' as awd some tickets gan me for to sell,
Aw coed tother neet an geet on very well.

John Seddon, Esq., is a daycent sort too,
He awlus supports me wen aw get up a doo ;
"The Firs" wur th' fust place at which aw did co',
An' what tickets he purchast th' committee weel know.

Messrs. Beazer an' Gilroy this season aw foind,
Have subscribed each a guinea, which shows they are
    koind ;
An' the Rev. R. Walmsley, awm happy to tell,
Has sent in a handsome donation as well.

An' last, tho' not th' least is Mesthur R. Platt,
Whoa's dun mi o'th printin' an chargt nowt for that
Every member, awm sure, ull be glad wen aw say,
For this grand entertainment they've nothin' to pay.

So neaw folks aw think its quite toime for to stop,
An' let th' next performer step into mi shop ;
Becose there's a lengthy programme to get throo,
Theerfore aw'll retire and bid yo' adew.

LINES COMPOSED AND RECITED

FOR THE JUVENILE MEMBERS OF ST. JOHN THE
BAPTIST BRANCH OF THE CHURCH OF ENGLAND
TEMPERANCE SOCIETY, NEW SPRINGS, ASPULL, ON
JANUARY 20TH, 1879.

NOW all you little boys and girls,
    Attention pay to me ;
And I will tell you what to do,
For our Society.

First, those of you who've signed the pledge,
Pray to the Lord your friend ;
For strength that you may keep the same,
Henceforth unto the end.

Each one of you may then expect,
Assistance from above ;
Because He's promised to help all,
Who ask in faith and love.

Next, try to get your little friends,
These meetings to attend ;
And help the New Springs Temperance Branch,
Its good work to extend.

We want the young especially,
To join our happy band,
That with their efforts we may bring,
The drink trade to a stand.

Although our meetings are but small,
And members rather few ;
Let's hope that God will bless the work,
We've now engaged to do.

The movement is a worthy one,
You'll readily confess ;
Therefore I want each one to try,
And make it a success.

It has been done in other towns,
And why not at New Springs?
My dear friends, is it not time—
To change the state of things?

Just look around and you will see,
Much sad and sore distress ;
Still public houses do increase,
Oh ! would that they were less.

'Twas only yesterday I saw,
While walking down Calc Lane ;
A notice fixed upon a door,
Which told me very plain,

An application would be made
In a fortnight or so ;
For another out-door license,
And 'twill be got also.

New spirit vaults are being made,
In country and in town ;
I wish our high authorities,
Would put such places down.

Thousands are dressed in rags to-day,
And sadly short of bread ;
Who might had they but kept off drink,
Been better clothed and fed.

Great praise is due to Mr. James,
I'm sure you'll all admit ;
For thus commencing this grand cause,
That we might benefit.

He's labour'd hard day after day,
This object to attain ;
Then let us help him all we can,
Because its for our gain.

John Christopher you'll understand,
Deserves our thanks as well ;
For all his able services,
Which few men could excel.

Really friends I cannot tell,
Whatever we should do ;
Did he not come and kindly help,
This new work to get through.

So now my little folks farewell,
Perhaps some future time ;
I may write you a piece again,
When we've got more to sign.

A TORY SONG.

FOR THE WIGAN PARLIAMENTARY ELECTION, 1880.

Tune—" When Johnny comes marching home."

NEAW lads, wen yo' begin to feight,—beware!
      beware!
Think what was done i' Sixty-eight, unfair! unfair!
      Deawn 'ith pits bi a well known mon,
      Just for th' sake of his brother John,
Who upset eawr Tory men on the votin' day.

Boath Lancaster and Woods wur sent— thro' that!
   thro' that!
Eawr good owd teawn to represent—an sat! an sat!
      Until Eighteen-seventy-four,
      Wen two stanch Tories wur sent o'er,
Wich made the Radikils look pale, as they went
   merchin home.

Lindsay an' Knowles ar' worthy men; an' true! an
   true!
If yo' don't send 'em back agen—yo'll rue! yo'll rue
      So from this moment knock abeawt,
      Vote for th' Tories an' keep th' Whigs eawt;
Then we'll sing gay wen Johnny goes marchin' 'ome.

They ar' the men to hav' a place—becose! becose!
Thro' um we're means cawr meight to raise—an'
    clothes! an' clothes!
        While t'other two aw'll bet a creawn,
        Spend hardly owt for th' good o'th' teawn;
These ar' things to ponder o'er afore the polling day.

Kurnel Corquodale con't win—awm sure! awm sure
He would look better givin' the tin—to th' poor, to
    th' poor.
        One would think th' chap owt to hav' sense
        To keep away au' save th' expense,
Which he will surely hav' to pay wen the job is o'er.

Do, bless yo lads, bi firm, aw pray—to th' end! to
    th' end!
So that true blue's may win the day—an' send! an
    send!
        The same two gentlemen once more.
        Yo'll find 'em trusty to the core;
An' we'll all sing gay wen the Whigs go merchin'
    home.

LINES ON A VISIT TO LUNNUN.

NEAW foak iv yo'll gi mi a bit o' yoar toime,
 Aw'll spin a short ditty i' Lankyshur rhoime ;
Abeawt th' last wick's visit to Lunnun's big teawn,
Wheer things surproist mi as aw rode up an' deawn.

Aw left mi owd derlin' an' th' childer o reet,
At a very strange heawr, an' travelt i'th' neet ;
Becose iv yo' book to goo bi a chep trip,
Yo mun bi theer i' toime or gi some one a tip.

Train started fro Wiggin a bit afore two,
An' in a short toime aw wur landed at Crewe ;
Wheer lots left ther placcs refreshments to get,
Whoile eawr owd iron hoss his whistle did wet.

Then wi seet off agen an' kept peggin away,
Till Staffort wur rowt, wheer sum chaps soakt ther
  clay ;
An' aw cud ha' done wi a bit ov a drain,
But cud'nt get sarvt, so aw went back to th' train.

Aw had a wee drop o' stuff in a bottle,
An' neaw an' then peawrt a sope deawn i' mi throttle,
Just to prevent one fro catchin' a cowd,
Wich trav'lers ar' subjekt to wen growin owd.

Aw wur welly done up wen aw geet to th' fur end,
Wheer aw happent to meet Robert Selkirk, mi' frend ;
Whoa wur koindly waitin' at th' stashun for me,
An' sed whoile aw stopped his guest aw mut be.

Wi geet a good breakfast, a wash, an' seet eawt,
For th' grand Crystal Palace an' lookt reawnd abeawt ;
It's a wunderful place an' whot aw see theer,
Aw raly con't tel, but a bit yo shall hear.

Mesther Manns, wur conductin' an orchestra fine,
Toole actin' an engineman off the line ;
Madame Patey, Foli, an' two other hands,
Wur singin' assisted bi three fust class bands.

Dinnie, the Scotchman sum gud feats did show,
Aw tawkt to a diver i'th' water below,
Th' visitors chuckt coppers in for a little fun ;
Wen they'd done aw axt him to ston a glass ov rum.

Th' chap know'd very weel aw wanted nowt o'th'
    sooart ;
Wi wur but simply tawkin' to cause a bit o' spoart ;
Still aw didn't work for nowt—J. Brooks gi mi a
    book ;
Iv yo want to see it coe at eawr heawse au look.

Sum four hundred steps aw next climbt iv not more,
An' lookt through mi glass the vast landskape o'er ;
Then sharply made back i'th' insoide for mi tay,
Bowt a few bits o' things an' then left for that day.

Aw turnt eawt o' Tewsday wi' mi hert ful o' glee,
To coe on mi koind friend, Lord Lindsay, M.P. ;
His heawse is i' Brook-street, an' wen aw knockt at
    th' door
It wur very soon answert bi' Benjamin Moor.

Whoa laft an' then sed cum forward this way,
I am certain I've seen your face up at Haigh.
His Lordship just then at his breakfast wur sat,
So the butler an' me had a bit ov a chat.

Wen breakfust wur o'er he went up to his room,
Towd him aw're deawn stairs an he sent for me soon ;
Neaw judge mi surproise wen he shook mi bi'th'
    hond,
An' made mi sit deawn though aw wanted to stond.

Then he said I am glad to see you here, Brown,
Is there anything I can do for you in town ;
Aw towd him it wud be a rich trayt to me,
Iv through th' heawse o' Perliment aw cud get to see.

So he sent deawn an' wrote eawt an order for two,
'Cose aw towd him James Ashton wud like to look
    through ;
Here's also another one for Thursday's debate ;
It's spechully for you Brown, so aw went theer i'
    state.

His Lordship then gi' mi a neat little book,
A work ov his own yo con coe in an' look.
He also has written mi name i'th' insoide,
An' as lung as aw liv' aw shal look on't wi proide.

Aw thankt him koindly for conductin' mi through,
His fancy workshop durin' mi interview ;
An' explainin' sum wheels he had recently made,
Wich no deawbt wud hav' put lots o' litters i'th'
    shade.

Now, Brown, said his Lordship, what more can I do ?
Well, mi Lord, aw shud proise yoar likeness, that's
    true ;
But th' perty whoa keeps em wur cawt on that day,
So he promist to send mi one over to Haigh.

Mesther Hands, whoa resides up i' Berkley Square,
An' keeps a respektable hostelry there ;
Treated mi th' same as iv awd bin his pet,
Sich koindness as that one shudno forget.

Aw seed sum grand places an' went in a few ;
For yoar informashun aw'll name one or two ;
The British Museum an' Kensington, too,
Ar' wuth onyone's whoile to hav' a peep through.

They chergt mi a bob for admishun to'th' Teawer,
Wheer a warder explaint things for welly an heawr ;
Abuv one hundred theawsand guns he did say,
Wur actily stored i'th' buildin' that day.

Th' Nashunal Gallery's a very noice seet,
Its collecshun o' picters afford a rich treat ;
An' whot's best ov o' yoan nothin' to pay,
So don't miss this shop wen passin' that way.

Through Westminster Abbey an' also St. Paul's,
Aw've passed once or twoice an' examin't the walls ;
Wheer lots o' grand moniments ar' to be seen,
Ov brave men who've fowt for ther country an'
          Queen.

Whoile i'th' grand Cathedral a tanner aw spent,
An' abuv' th' whisp'rin gallery made an ascent ;
Thinks I to misel' aw'll be a greight mon,
An' whoile up at Lunnun see o' as aw con.

Awve not towd yo o', aw cud tel yo sum more,
But awm sure yo'll admit it's quite toime to giv o'er ;
An' iv ever aw goo i' that querter agen,
Aw'll gi' yo' another rough sketch fro mi pen.

LINES ON MY FIRST APPEARANCE
IN WIGAN.

WEN penny readin's fust begun,
  Aw thowt awd try mi hand ;
An' use whot talent aw possest,
Throoeawt mi native land.

Awst ne'er forget th' fust toime aw read,
I' Wiggin Publick Ho' ;
An' iv mi memory is corrokt ;
Its sixteen yers ago.

William Hardy read th' same neet,
An' T. R. Ellis too ;
They very soon put me i'th' shade,
Mark ! whot aw say is true.

But then aw ne'er wur sent to th' schoo',
Eawr foak wur very poor ;
Mi feyther'd but twelve bob a wick,
To keep him and six moor.

Some toimes mi mother workt a bit,
For Hill at th' Standish Ho' ;
Or else wi never could hav' lived,
An' paid th' heawse rent an' o.

Ther wur but one schoo' near eawr heawse,
Towt by a Mesthur Price;
His son resides i'th' village neaw,
An' doin' very nice.

Iv awd gone to that grammar skoo,
An' larnt o'th subjeks throo,
Aw shud'nt hav' bin Dick Deadeye neaw—
Praps th' captain o' some crew.

Heawever foalk aw'll not complain,
At mi low posishun;
Theawsands o' eddykated men,
Ar' in a wuss condishun.

Wen Ralph Darlington coed o' me,
To read a funny tale;
From th' pen o' my friend Brierley,
Whoas pieces never fail.

Some young fellows whoa stood at th' dur,
 Begun to laff at me;
But after o' aw sarvt um cawt,
An' that yo'll quickly see.

Afore awd gotten hawve way throo',
Some twenty-foive or six;
Kept neaw an' then strikin' th' floor,
 Wi canes an' fancy sticks.

Mi subjekt certainly wur lung,
An' it had gotten late ;
But th' Cheermon sed ne'er heed um Brown,
I'm willin' for to wait.

So aw kept on an' read th' piece throo',
An' after it wur o'er ;
Some applause were given to me,
An' one fop sed onkoro.

Mony a chap would ne'er hav' read,
Another piece agen ;
But aw're determint to keep on
An' conquer sich like men.

Though aw made a very bad start,
Success is drawin' near;
Its only whot one may expect,
Iv he'll but persevere.

Two men wur in the theatre,
Wen aw wur axt to sing ;
A song which caused the audience,
To make th' owd buildin' ring.

Eh ! what a different meetin',
Thoose gentlemen would see ;
Compared wi that i'th' Publick Ho',
Wen each one fust yerd me.

In fact one ov um sed th' same neet,
In the Royal Hotel;
Your tory song pleased me the best,
Becose yo did it well.

Drink up an' hav' a glass wi' me,
My good friend, H. did say ;
For which aw thank't him an' then sed,
Yes sir, some other day.

So neaw young men wen yo' begin,
Some useful work, and good,
Don't be put deawn bi ony one,
Act loike bowd Robin Hood.

LINES COMPOSED AND GIVEN IN

MR. CHARLIE KEITH'S CIRCUS,

ON THE EVENING OF HIS BENEFIT.

LADIES an' gentlemen, please excuse,
 My comin' here yo' to amuse,
Becose aw think that ev'ry mon
Shud do a good turn wen he con.

No deawt yo'd loike to see Jim Brown
Act in this circus loike a clown ;
Wouldn't it be rare fun for you ?
But that aw don't profess to do.

Friend Keith, one Saturday at noon,
Axt me i' Mester Best's front room,
If awd recoite or sing a bit,
On the night of his benefit.

Yes, wi' my employers' consent,
Who wouldn't refuse if aw wur bent ;
After wich aw yerd nowt more
Till th' last wick's papper wur lookt o'er.

When aw fust read mi name i' print,
Up th' office steps aw made a sprint,
To ax mi mesther his advice,
He allus deals wi me so nice.

Well, he said, you'd best go down,
Becose you're well known thro' the town,
An' give a song or recitation
For the people's delectation.

Aw spoke to Charlie Keith th' same night,
Who said he thought that all was right,
Or he wouldn't have used my name;
Neaw yo' con choose where lies the blame.

He's on a greight expense, no deawt,
An' soon may have to clear cawt;
Therefore, he's anxious to get gain,
Whoile i' Wiggin he does remain.

Aw' dunnot wish to do th' chap harm,
Though someone's made my shop so warm;
May success his travels attend,
Till his circus is at an end.

He caters weel yo'll o admit,
An' owt to reap some benefit;
Splendid talent he engages,
Which must cost enormous wages.

His performers are o' clever,
Some as popular as ever;
One or two aw'll try to menshun,
If yo'll kindly give attenshun.

Madame Gilbert aw loike to see.
Hoo rides an' acts so gracefully,
No matter whether on horse or feet,
Hur actions are to me a treat.

Aw munnot forget Miss Marguerite,
Hur stoile o' ridin' suits me quite.
Especially in that Swiss scene,
Wich hoo goos throo' so neat an' clean.

George Gilbert does some darin' tricks,
It's astonishin' heaw th' chap sticks;
Whoile the horse is gallopin reawnd
He jumps straight up on't from the greawnd.

Carter and Douglas both ride well,
Wi more whose names aw' connot tell.
An' Mrs. Keith aw loike to see,
Who on the tight rope pleases me.

Erno and Onzo's antics please,
Booath are awhoam on the trapeze;
Besoides they're funny lookin' chaps,
An' keep hittin' each other raps.

Little Lizzie's work aw admire,
The girl's so young to walk on wire,
Though her daddy stands by hur side
Watchin' hur little footsteps glide.

Charlie Keith, yo' mun understand,
Performs a trick on his right hand
Which aw've never seen done before,
Aw coo it swimmin' on the shore.

Each of those three lads are clever,
There equals, friends, aw've seen never ;
Would it not be a greight disgrace
If in my lines they'd not a place ?

Nimse, who acts as Keith's stud groom
Does his part in another room,
And judgin' from each horse's state,
The man acquits himself first-rate.

Bianchi and his splendid band,
Discourse some fust-class music grand ;
Therefore aw'll give to them their due,
Becose whot aw neaw say is true.

There's Chapman, too, plays well his part,
He seems to have it off by heart,
Few ringmasters can him excel,
So neaw aw'll stop an' say farewell.

COMPOSED AND R CITED AT

LEIGH WORKHOUSE,

ON THE OCCASION OF THE ANNUAL TREAT, GIVEN BY

J. H. NICHOLS, ESQ., TO THE INMATES,

JANUARY 1ST, 1881.

WELL foak awm gradely glad to see
    Yo'n bin sar'vt wi a rare good tea,
Throo a gentlemen aw well know
God bless him an' his wife also.

Aw once fill'd a situation
Under him at Wiggin Station ;
He wur th' goods agent at that time
On the owd North Union line.

A better mester aw ne'er had,
He never sauced or said owt bad,
An' wen aw chanced to do owt wrung
He alus spoke mild wi his tung.

Though twenty yers hav' past an' gone,
He's here th' fust day i' eighty one ;
Lets hope he'll live o'er twenty moor,
An' show th' same charity to th' poor.

Its not th' fust time, aw understand,
That he's stretched forth his lib'ral hand
In order to provide some cheer
For o yo' inmates each new year.

His better hawve, aw mun confess,
Has striven hard an' gain'd success ;
Wen mon an' wife together poo
A fortune they deserve that's true.

Aw ne'er thowt afore their marriage,
They'd keep sich a hoss an' carriage
As that in wich aw've had a ride
Fro' Lowton Church Schoo to Parkside.

Wheer his residence, Sandfield Ho,
Is situated, yo' shud coo !
Moi word it is a bonny place,
An' wouldn't a lord or earl disgrace.

Awm sure yo'll o' wi me agree
He's just th' rect mon for a J.P.,
As well as guardian of the poor,
Whoa Lowton foak shud keep secure.

If they dunnot aw deawt they'll rue,
Becose he's genuine an' true ;
His splendid treats each newyer's day
Will bear me cawt in whot aw say.

May peace an' plenty him attend,
An' blessin's from on high descend
Upon him an' his worthy wife,
Throoeawt this sinful mortal life.

An' wen life's battles here are o'er,
May they both meet to pert no more
In that breet mansion up abuv,
Where all is joy, an' peace, an' luv.

THE PEMBERTON LIBRARY EPISODE.

AW took up yoar papper last wick,
 A few little bits to glance o'er,
An' wurn't aw surproised for to see
 That meetin' which cawst sich uproar.

An as aw're bin axt bi sum friends
 To put a few verses i' rhoime
Abeawt the disgraceful affair
 Aw'll do so, though stinted for toime.

Directly the schoo' clock struck seven,
 H. Widdows geet up to propose
That owd fermer Whoite shud tak th' cheor
 Until the proceedins did close.

Wich sum mon soon jumPt up to secund,
 His name they coed Yetton, aw think,
An' judgin' fro' th' chap's windy talk,
 Aw guess he'd had summat to drink.

Beawt puttin the moshun to th' meetin'
 Owd Whoite at once popt into th' chair,
Afore Mester Barrett* arroived,
 Wich yo mun admit were unfair.

   * Chairman of the Local Board, Pemberton.

The Local Board foak wur axt fust
    A ratepayer's meetin' t' convene,
Then why not let th' reet un presoide ?
    For shame on yo actin so mean.

Whoite owt to ha' shift o' one soide,
    An gan Mester Barrett his place ;
Things wud ha' gone far better on,
    Besoides lesseuin' th' shame an disgrace.

*Partington seem'd quite astonish'd,
    An' hardly cud tell whot to do ;
Whoile Barrett an' o his supporters
    Appeart likewoise in a stew.

†Charnock, fro' Wiggin, spoke cawt plain,
    An' towd 'em regardless o' feor,
His candid opinion wur,
    That Barrett shud ockipy th' cheor.

Heawever, it o' wur no use,
    They couldn't get owd Whoite to stur ;
Theerfore, they had no other plan
    But to tak matters just as they wur.

Aw'm towd sum o'th' roughs wur quite fresh,
    Not wi drinkin' hot coffee an' tay,
But sum nowty stuff wich it seems,
    Droives senses an' rayson away.

    * Clerk of the Local Board.   † Their Lawyer's Clerk.

Neaw, iv the report be o' true,
   An' there is no occashun to deawt,
Why didn't thoose greenhorns ger up,
   Put their hats on, au' then walk reet eawt ?

Heaw con the owd village improve
   Wi sich stormy meetings as that ?
Neaw, moind yo iv they dunnot rue
   Sum day wen it's happen too late.

A big B aw'm glad did attend,
   Still th' swarm only made twenty-foive ;
Neaw, whot cud thoose few warkers do
   Wi' two hundred drones keawrt i'th' hoive ?

One little un stuck loike a " Leech,"*
   An' browt sum grand matter to bear
In order to get the Acts pass'd,
   But the numskulls, yo see, didn't care.

Heaw cud thoose bad fellows, for shame,
   That koind little mon to abuse
Whoile doin' his utmost to get
   Each workin' mon's childer chep news?

It shows whot an ignorant lot
   Wur pack'd into th' schoo'reawm that neet ;
They cudn't ha' carried on wuss
   If raly they had bin noan reet.

* Wm. Leech, Esq., Member of the Local Board.

When Barrett stud up on his feet
  He spoke loike a sensible chap,
But ere he had said mony words
  The cheorman hit him a hard rap.

Mester Alker* did o' he could,
  An' made a foine offer besoide,
Wich aw see they wud not accept.
  He had to sit deawn an' aboide.

Aw'm glad to see James Moss wur woise,
  An' wish aw cud say th' same for Bill,
Becose it hurts me, dun yo see,
  To tawk o' mi nayburs so ill.

All honour to thoose twenty-foive
  For tryin to pass a good skame,
Wich wud hav browt credit to th' parish,
  Instead o' so very mich blame.

If the Libraries' Acts didn't pass,
  Aw'm sertin that sum could be made
Wich wud pleos foak reawnd abeawt here,
  Th' promoters wud droive a rare trade.

Whot sen yo, lads, shud wi just try
  To ger up a bit ov a do,
Aw know one who wud prepare th' piece,
  An' help us to act a bit too.

  *Edward Alker, Esq., a Member of the Local Board.

Eh! shudn't wi hav lots o' sport,
　It wud be a capital trick;
Aw'll promis' to act Billy Moss,
　An' knock abeawt th' stage wi a stick.

After o', chaps, it wudn't be rect
　To carry the lark quite so far;
Then let's hope they'll grow woiser men,
　An' leave matters just as they are.

SUBSCRIBERS.

Ackerley, Henry, Wigan
Ainsworth, Henry, Haigh
Airey, T., Wigan
Anderton, E. W., Hindley
Appleton, C., Greenhill, Wigan
Arnott, W. H., Laurel House, Lowton
Atherton, T., Poplar House, Hindley

Baldwin, John, 6, Park View, Wigan
Barker, W., Little Scotland, Blackrod
Barlow, Daniel, Wigan
Barlow, J. E., Wigan
Barlow, Robt., Wigan
Barnish, Dr., Wigan
Barrett, W. S., Liverpool
Berry, Wm., Surgeon. Wigan
Blaylock, Councillor, Wigan
Bolton, W., Borough Engineer, Wigan
Boydell, James, Farnworth
Bradley, Robt., Parbold
Brandreth, James, Warrington
Bridgeman, Hon. & Rev. Canon, The Hall, Wigan.
Brookes, E., Standish
Brown, W. D., Wigan
Browne, John, Wigan
Bryan, Rev. W. B., the Vicarage, Haigh
Bryham, John, Ince
Bryham, W., Ince Hall
Bryham, W. jun., Pagefield, Wigan
Byrom, Alderman, Wigan

Campbell, G. L., Wigan
Carey, J. Williamson, Wigan
Chadwick, W., Standish.
Chalk, W., Moorland House, Aspull
Charlson, T., Wigan
Christopher, R., Ince
Clark, C. F., Cranbury Lodge, Wigan
Cockson, C., Wigan
Coombs, Dr., Wigan

Crankshaw, W., Standish
Crawford and Balcarres, Rt. Hon. Earl of, Haigh Hall
Crawshaw, C., Minorca Hotel, Wigan
Cronshaw, Rev. J., St. Thomas', Wigan

Darlington, James, Meriden Hall, Coventry
Darlington, H., Wigan
Darlington, Ralph, Wigan
Dean, B. G., Wigan
Dean, W., Hindley
Dickinson, Geo, Leigh
Dobb, Dr., Brooklands, Golborne
Dorrian, James, J.P., Bolton

Eckersley, N., J.P., Standish Hall
Edwardson, James, J.P., Wigan
Entwisle, R. H., Holmes House, Blackrod
Evans, Rev. A., Grammar School, Wigan
Fergie, Rev. Canon, Ince.

Fair, J. W., Lytham
Farington, Ald., J.P., Mariebonne, Wigan.
Finch, G. B., 24, Old Square, Lincoln's Inn, London.
Fitzadam, J. T., 5, Phillimore Gardens, Kensington, London, W.C.
Forster, W., Millgate, Wigan
France, W. S., J.P., Wigan
Gardner, John, Castlefield House, Blackrod
Gaskell, W., Southport
Gee, Councillor, Wigan.
Gerrard, Councillor, Wigan
Gilroy, G., Hindley Hall
Gray, W, 214, Piccadilly, London
Green, Thomas, Wigan Lane, Wigan
Greener, W. J., Pemberton
Griffith, H., Wigan
Grime, W., Wigan.
Grundy, John, Rose Hill House, Hindley

Hains, Rev. P., St. George's, Wigan
Hall, Dr., Ince
Halliwell, Councillor, Wigan
Halliwell, John, Bury
Halliwell, R., Wigan
Hands, Alfred, Berkeley Square, London
Harbottle, W. H., Latham House, Orrell
Hardy, W., Wigan.
Hawkins, J. G., Gas Manager, Wigan
Hayes, James, West Leigh House, W'leigh
Headd, T., Wigan
Heaton, Reuben, Wigan
Hewlett. A., J.P., Haseley Manor, near
    Warwick
Hewlett, W.H , Strickland House, Standish
Heyes, Councillor, Wigan
Hill and Schofield, Wigan
Hilton, Councillor, Wigan
Hilton, J., Longhurst, Haigh
Hilton, T. W., F.G S., Holly Bank, Haigh
Hodgson, James, Ulverston
Holding, W., Stapleford, nr. Nottingham
Holmes, C. B., Wigan
Holmes, James, Wigan
Holt, W., Borough Treasurer, Wigan
Hopwood, Alderman, Wigan
Hornby, James, Wigan
Horrocks, Wright, Worthington
Hubbert, Z., Wigan
Hurst, James, Wigan

Jackson, Superintendent, Leigh
Jagger, John, Hindley
Johnson, J. H., Southport
Johnson, W., Crown Inn, Aspull
Jolley, R. & W., Wigan

Kay, James, Rose Mount, Coppull
Kennion, Captain, Chief Constable, Wigan
Kent, S., Ashton-on-the-Ribble, nr. Preston
Kirk, Dr., Hindley
Knowles, Israel, Ince
Knowles, T., M.P., Wigan

Lamb, J. and Co., Wigan

Lamb, W. J., J.P., the Sycamores, Wigan
Lawrence, E., Know Farm, Euxton
Lea, Councillor R., Wigan
Leigh, John, Gidlow Hall, Aspull
Leyland, John, J.P., the Grange, Hindley
Lindsay, Colin, J.P., Deer Park, Honiton,
    Devon
Litherland, Henry, Wigan
Lowe, John, Workhouse, Wigan

Makinson, G., Colinfield, Wigan
Makinson, John, Upholland
Mapei, L. V., East Bank, Golborne
Marsh, John, Grove Terrace, Adlington
Marsh, W , Holly House, Hindley
Mawson, J. Y., Wigan
Mayhew, H., J.P., Bank House, Wigan
Mayhew, W., The Woodlands, Wigan
Meaden, Samuel, Wigan
Meek, J. and Sons, Wigan
Millington, Alfred, Wigan
Mitchell, W., Brook Villa, Golborne
Molyneux, Dr., Upholland
Moss, Enoch, Broad Oak, Rossett, near
    Wrexham
Moor, Benjamin, 47, Brook-St., London

Nevill, J., J.P., Southport
Nichols, J. H., Sandfield Hall, Newton-le-
    Willows
Nixon, Jas., Hindley

Occleshaw, John, Hindley
Oldfield, Councillor, Wigan
Ormrod, Thomas, Southport

Park, H., J.P., Southport
Parker, C., 6, Strand, London, W.C.
Part, Thomas, Aldenham Lodge, Watford
Peace, M. W., Ashfield, Standish
Pearce, J. Worth, Clarendon House, Eccles
Pearson, John, J.P., Golborne Park
Pendlebury, John, J.P., Wigan
Pennington, R. jun., J.P., Muncaster Hall,
    Rainford

Percy, C. M., F.G.S., The Grove, Standish
Phillips, J., Wigan
Pickard, W., Wigan
Pickering, J., Fisher House, Orrell
Pigot, Rev. O. F., Chaplain's House, Kirkdale
Platt, Councillor R., Wigan
Platt, Councillor W., Wigan
Powell, F. S., M.P., Horton Old Hall, near Bradford
Preston, John, Wigan
Price, Dr., Standish

Quirk, Rev. T. C., The Vicarage, Golborne
Rawcliffe, H., Euxton Hall, Nr. Chorley
Rawson, H. E., Moat House, Haigh
Rigby, W., Hindley
Rimmer, Nathan, Wigan
Robinson, Thomas, Westleigh
Roocroft, Dr , Wigan
Rose, Josiah, Chronicle Office, Leigh
Rowbottom, Major, Coroner, Wigan

Rowland, S., Wigan
Scarborough, G., Wigan
Seddon, John, The Firs, Aspull
Seddon, R. B., Ince
Selkirk Robert, Battersea
Shepherd, Dr., Wigan
Shortrede, T., Winstanley
Shuttleworth, Joseph, Hindley
Simm, G. S., Poolstock, Wigan
Simm, Wm , Frodsham, Cheshire
Smith, Alderman, Wigan
Smith, Councillor James, J.P., Wigan
Smith, H., Acresfield House, Blackrod
Smith, John, Bickershaw House, Abram
Southworth, Thomas, Laurel House, Hindley
Spencer, Robert, Blackburn
St. George, Rev. H., M.A., J.P., Billinge
Stone, T. H , G, Wigan Lane, Wigan
Strickland, W., Wigan
Swan, W., Wigan
Swift, T. D., Moat House, Ince
Swire, Samuel, Crown House, Southport

Tarbuck, John, Tyldesley
Tarbuck, Joseph, Wigan
Tarbuck, Wm., Wigan
Taylor, T. R , Wigan
Tickle Brothers, Ironfounders, Wigan
Topping, Councillor, Wigan
Topping, W., Bamfurlong
Twynem, R. C., 174, Islington, L'pool
Tyrer, Peter, 70, Long Lane, London. S.E.
Tyrer, Thos., Standishgate, Wigan

Unwin, Dr., Wigan

Waddington, W., Thornhill, Standish
Wall, T., J.P., Wallgate, Wigan
Walls, H., Derby Terrace, Hindley
Walls, John, Wigan
Walmsley, Rev. R., Pennington Green
Waugh, Edwin, Kersal Hotel, near Manchester
Webster, A. E., Charnock Vicarage, near Chorley
Whitfield, J., Dicconson Street, Wigan
Wigan Free Library, per H. T. Folkard, Librarian
Wigan Examiner, per W. Roger
Wigan Observer, per C. Wall
Wilcock, George, Hall Green House, Upholland
Wilding, W., Ince
Williams, J. B., Liverpool
Winnard, J., Newburgh
Winnard, W., Wigan
Winstanley, John, Orrell
Wilson, T., 20, Swinley Terrace, Wigan
Wood, Councillor, Wigan
Wood, F., Wigan
Wood, J. A., Wigan
Woodcock, H. S., J.P., The Elms, Wigan
Woodcock, R. Fraser, Wigan
Wright, H. E., Wigan
Wright, Jno., Eaton Hall, Chester

Yates, Christopher, Preston
Yates, John, Wigan
Yates, John, Fazackerley Street, Chorley

WIGAN:

Printed by Richard Platt, 2, Standishgate.

Works : Millgate and Wiend.

1881.

www.ingramcontent.com/pod-product-compliance
Lightning Source LLC
Chambersburg PA
CBHW022153020726
47496CB00008B/2687